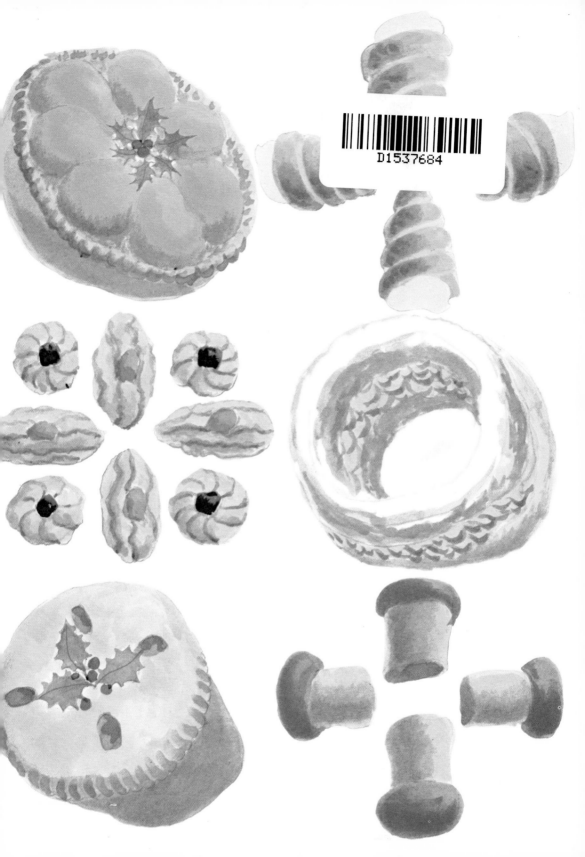

Mother Goose for Christmas

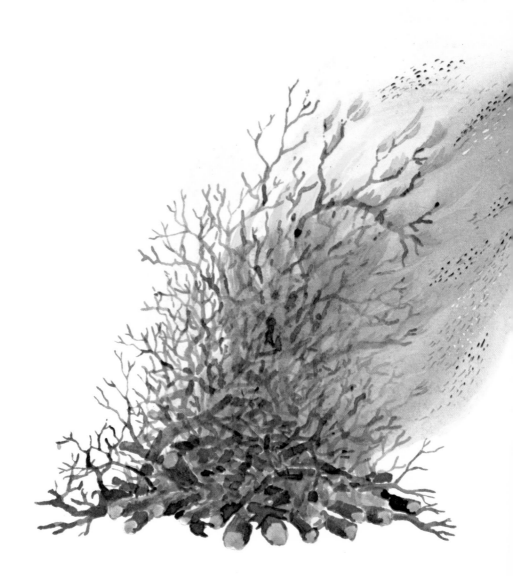

William Pène du Bois

MOTHER GOOSE
for Christmas

The Viking Press   New York

Also by William Pène du Bois

Bear Circus	Otto in Texas
Otto and the Magic Potatoes	Otto at Sea
Elisabeth the Cow Ghost	Lion
Bear Party	The Giant
The Three Little Pigs	Peter Graves
Otto in Africa	The Twenty-One Balloons
The Three Policemen	The Great Geppy

First Edition

Copyright © 1972, 1973, by William Pène du Bois. All rights reserved. First published in 1973 by The Viking Press, Inc., 625 Madison Avenue, New York, N.Y. 10022. Published simultaneously in Canada by The Macmillan Company of Canada Limited. Library of Congress catalog card number: 72-91406   1 2 3 4 5 77 76 75 74 73

Pic Bk

SBN 670-49007-5   PRINTED IN U.S.A.

Pour Jackie,
Karine et Flynn

Christmas was coming, the geese were getting fat. Pennies were jingling in the old man's hat. Everyone in the village was thinking of having a happy time.

It was a cozy village.

The sky was clear, and there was a fresh white coat of deep squeaky snow.

The houses were fat and warm under thick blankets of straw. Their walls seemed to bulge from all the pease porridge, roasts, hot buttered beans, tarts, and pies that went through every door. Dogs were spoiled, pussy cats sat by the fire. Pipers piped and fiddlers fiddled and children sang a lot.

7

The villagers were famous all over the world.

It was a rare place in which to live. It didn't have a policeman and didn't seem to need one.

What made this village particularly fine was that it was the home of Mother Goose, the poet. She lived, with her big Goosey Gander, in a bookstore on the corner. There was a nursery and a nice big yard out back where children were left on days when their mothers were too busy to care for them properly. The villagers all knew and loved Mother Goose because she had looked after each of them at some time or other in her nursery. She would write poems about them that made them laugh. They were all grateful to her, because the poems she wrote had made them famous.

Then something terrible happened.

It was the day before Christmas. Little Tommy Tucker saw it happen, and when he told all the villagers about it, he was in a dreadful state. "There were two men— not from *our* village, mind you—two strangers."

"What were they like?" asked Jack Sprat.

"Well, one was tubby, wearing checkered trousers and a white coat smeared with red spots."

"Smeared with red spots!" echoed the villagers.

"And the other"—Georgy Porgy piped up—"just how was he put together?"

"Ever so stupid-looking," said Little Tommy Tucker. "All loose arms and legs, and a big mouth that hung open —full of teeth."

"Gracious me!" gasped Little Miss Muffet. She fainted dead away. Tom Tom, the piper's son, patted her cheeks and revived her.

"Were they hurting Mother Goose?" asked Little Bo-Peep, herself wearing a face screwed up with pain.

"It was hard to tell. At the time, it was more Goosey Gander I was worried about. They'd put a rope around his neck, and he was honking something fierce. The fat one was tugging him with one hand, with his other squeezed around Mother Goose's wrist."

"What was the stupid one up to?" asked Little Bo-Peep, covering her pet lamb's ears so it might not be shocked.

"The stupid one followed close behind, a huge bag slung over his shoulders, drool spilling from his toothy mouth," said Little Tommy Tucker.

"Mercy!" Old Mother Hubbard muttered. Her dog started growling. She sent him off to play.

"The saddest part—" Little Tommy Tucker continued (he seemed to be fighting back tears), "the saddest part was that Mother Goose was reciting a new poem. As I remember, it went something like this:

Christmas comes but once a year,

And when it comes it brings good cheer."

Hearing these lines was a bit too much for Mother Goose's friends. They started crying, and their sobbing was as loud as it was unashamed.

"Only Mother Goose," said the little girl with the curl, her face wet with tears, "could recite such dear verse at a time like that!"

"Where did they take them?" asked Little Jack Horner, wiping his apple cheeks with the back of his sleeve.

"To The Queen of Hearts," said Little Tommy Tucker.

"Why that bakery shop has been boarded up for months," said Jack Sprat.

"Ever since that summer's day when all the tarts were stolen clean away," Jack Sprat's wife agreed. "We haven't had a bakery since—more's the pity. I sure do miss it!"

"How did they get inside, if it's all boarded up?" No matter how Georgy Porgy put a question, he always made it seem unfriendly.

14

"The stupid one—" said Little Tommy Tucker, "he looked as strong as an ox. He put down his bag, yanked a board off the shutters, ripped them open, pushed his foot through a pane of glass, stuck in his hand, opened the window, threw in Goosey Gander, lifted in Mother Goose, wedged the fat one through, tossed in his bag, hopped in himself, slammed the shutters shut, closed the window, and started hammering from inside."

"Mercy!" repeated Old Mother Hubbard. "Mother Goose and Goosey Gander nailed in with two strangers!"

Without anyone's suggesting it, the group started walking off toward the boarded-up bakery shop. Each, at the time, seemed to think silence was important, and they crunched through the snow on tiptoes. Rounding the corner, they crept past the cemetery and up Pippen Hill. They wanted a good view from on high. Jill hung onto Jack, whose balance on tiptoes was poor, to say the least. When they reached the well on top of the hill, they stopped,

horrified. Black smoke, flaked with soot, was pouring from the bakery chimney.

"That fire is for burning Mother Goose!" said Little Boy Blue. It was a terrible thought which most of the friends seemed to share.

"For burning Mother Goose," a mournful chorus echoed.

"Not necessarily," said Mary Mary, quite contrary, "they could have started a fire because it's cold."

"It's for burning Mother Goose," repeated Little Boy Blue, who saw things on the sad side.

"Mary Mary could be right," said Jack Sprat. "The bakery has been boarded up for some time. The chimney needs cleaning. That could explain the black smoke."

"It's for burning Mother Goose," Little Boy Blue moaned softly.

"Stubborn boy," said Jack Sprat's wife. "Let's look at it this way. Christmas is tomorrow. Perhaps the men wanted goose for Christmas dinner. Perhaps they don't know how to roast a goose. Perhaps they found a goose and a lady to roast it for them—not to mention an empty house with a big oven. What do you say to that?"

"ROAST GOOSEY GANDER!" Everyone screamed in horror. The idea seemed as bad as burning Mother Goose.

"Oh, dear, what can we do?" asked the little girl with the curl.

"I have a plan," Jack, to whom Jill was still clinging, announced.

"What is it?" asked Georgy Porgy.

"My idea is simple. We must put out the fire in The Queen of Hearts. Without the fire they cannot keep warm, they cannot roast Goosey Gander, and they cannot burn

Mother Goose. I say put out the fire and keep it out."

"And just how would you do that?" asked Georgy Porgy.

"Jill and I will form a bucket brigade," Jack said, "from the well here to the chimney on top of The Queen of Hearts. We'll run up and down the hill, and up and down the roof, and keep pouring buckets of water in the chimney."

"You two are so good at fetching pails of water," said Georgy Porgy, his voice ending in high-pitched giggles.

"Others could help," Jill argued. "Even *you*."

But others didn't offer to help. They seemed to be afraid to go too near the bakery.

"What we really need is a policeman," said Little Bo-Peep. "Had we had a policeman at the time the tarts were stolen or, come to think of it," she added wistfully, "when I lost my sheep, we might not now find ourselves in this pickle."

"Where *is* the nearest policeman?" Georgy Porgy asked.

"There's a brave one in Babylon," Old Mother Hubbard answered.

"How many miles is it to Babylon?"

"Threescore miles and ten."

"Can I get there by candlelight?"

"Yes, and back again. . . ."

20

"Quiet!" Jack Sprat shouted. "This is no time for rhymes! It's a time for saving Mother Goose and Goosey Gander!"

"But I thought I'd run to Babylon for—"

"You're too fat to run to Babylon, Georgy Porgy," said Jack Sprat. "No. If we are to save Mother Goose and Goosey Gander, we must start doing it ourselves, here, and right away."

"Oh, but how?" asked the little girl with the curl. "It all seems so impossible."

"I don't quite know how," said Jack Sprat. "I thought Jack and Jill's idea of a bucket brigade was fine, but we're afraid to help them. We're afraid to put out the fire in The Queen of Hearts with buckets of water because we're afraid of being grabbed somehow and nailed up inside along with Mother Goose and Goosey Gander."

"That's right," said Little Miss Muffet. "That's exactly the way *I* feel."

The others made embarrassed grunts and nodded their heads. They were not a brave lot.

Little Tommy Tucker then did a strange thing. He placed his right hand on his heart and recited again the poem he had heard Mother Goose recite:

Christmas comes but once a year,
 And when it comes it brings good cheer.

He walked a few steps down the hill toward The Queen of Hearts. He paused and stared for some time at the boarded-up bakery. He then turned and faced the others. "I think I have it," he said. "The Christmas spirit! That's how we'll save them."

"What's *your* plan?" asked Georgy Porgy.

"We won't form a bucket brigade," said Little Tommy Tucker. "We'll form a Christmas carol brigade. We'll sing Christmas carols outside The Queen of Hearts in shifts, right up to Christmas and beyond. That's it! We'll melt their hearts. We'll sing day and night until they let Mother Goose and Goosey Gander go."

"Oh, that's a lovely idea," said Old Mother Hubbard. "Soften them up with Christmas carols."

"It might well work at that," said Jack Sprat. "It would be hard to wring a goose's neck—what with all the honking and messy business—while the sweet sounds of 'Silent Night' filled the air."

"And you hate goose," said Jack Sprat's wife.

"I like the plan too," said the old woman who lived in a shoe. "Who indeed could harm a dear lady like Mother Goose while young voices sing out, 'In that poor stable, how charming Jesus lies.'"

"I love it," said Little Bo-Peep.

"And they couldn't possibly get mad at us for singing Christmas carols," said Little Miss Muffet. "It just isn't done!"

"We'll get Tom Tom's father to play his pipes," said Little Jack Horner, "and Little Boy Blue can blow his horn."

"If it's not already too late," said Little Boy Blue.

"And we'll get that fine cat to play his fiddle," Little Jack Horner continued.

"Oh, I just know it's going to work," said Little Miss Muffet.

"Well of course, it just *has* to," said Jack Sprat. "It's

not a plan we can allow to fail. Are we all agreed to try it?"

Mother Goose's friends nodded their heads.

"It's not a bad plan at that," said Georgy Porgy, in a rare display of Christmas warmth.

After dividing themselves according to voice into four groups, the friends of Mother Goose and Goosey Gander started singing Christmas carols outside the boarded-up old bakery that was still belching black smoke.

It was a nice day before Christmas, and it promised to be a clear but chilly Christmas Eve. Big bonfires were lit on each side of The Queen of Hearts to keep the carolers warm. It made such a pretty, touching scene that the village animals found it hard to stay away. The cow who jumped over the moon was there, along with the laughing dog and Dickory Dickory Dare, the pig who flew up in the air. Pussy-cat Mew came too, but sat away from the bonfires. The ducks and drakes and donkeys came, and even the three blind mice were attracted by the singing. All sat quietly, as if they knew that Mother Goose and Goosey Gander were locked inside, and hoped that their presence might help make everything turn out all right.

As a bright red Christmas sun peeped over Pippen Hill, the singing became louder and louder. This was because the singers were too excited to go home when they were relieved, and they would simply round the corner of the bakery and continue singing there. In the lovely pink early daylight there was a group singing merrily on each side of The Queen of Hearts, and all the animals had closed in too, wide awake and watching.

Suddenly the smoke pouring from The Queen of Hearts chimney changed color. It had been thick, black, and sooty. Now it turned a nice blue-gray. Little Bo-Peep noticed it first. She sniffed and screamed right in the middle of "Hark, the Herald Angels Sing," "Good gracious! It smells of sugar and spice and everything nice!"

"That's what girls are made of!" Georgy Porgy bellowed.

"What does?" Little Jack Horner shouted.

"The smoke up there, and it's changed color!"

"They're burning Mother Goose!" shouted Little Boy Blue.

Little Miss Muffet fainted dead away. Tom Tom, the piper's son, revived her again by patting her cheeks.

"What will we do? Oh! *What* will we do?" moaned the old woman who lived in a shoe.

"Sing louder, sing merrier!" Jack Sprat yelled. "SING YOUR HEARTS OUT!"

Then banging started, loud and noisy pounding from upstairs. Boards loosened, then burst from the building. Shutters swung open, and there in a window stood the stupid one, a silly grin spread across his face. "Merry Christmas!" he shouted. He bowed and disappeared.

Then, immediately, more banging, and the shutters of
another window flew open. The tubby one appeared,
white coat covered with red smears. "Merry Christmas!"
he repeated with a bow. He too vanished.

The frightened singers were caroling merrier than ever.
"'Tis the season to be jolly!" they sang. Each one wore
a terrified expression.

One set of shutters after the other was flung apart. The carolers heard a thudding sound. The stupid one and the fat man had attacked the front door like a human battering ram. The door burst open, and boards flew in a shower of splinters, and there the kidnapers stood, cheek to cheek, their smiles making rows of huge teeth across their faces. "Merry Christmas!" they chorused. Then they bowed, turned, and ducked inside.

Frightful squawks came from upstairs in The Queen of Hearts. Goosey Gander was honking and thrashing and banging his wings. Then one of the kidnapers shouted, "You've got to go through with it, Goosey, it's Christmas Day!" There was the sound of a terrible slap.

"They're roasting Goosey Gander too!" cried Little Boy Blue.

"Sing, sing, SING!" Jack Sprat shouted. His face turned pale.

A loud and nervous sound of "Oh, come all ye faithful/ Joyful and triumphant!" filled the air, mixing with still more honks, slaps, and beating of wings, when—sight of sights—from an upstairs window of The Queen of Hearts flew Goosey Gander carrying Mother Goose on his back. The big dear bird swept low over the crowd with Mother

Goose laughing happily and shouting "MERRY CHRISTMAS!"
Over her left arm she had a wicker basket from which
she pelted her friends below with hot Christmas cookies.
"All of you go home and give your presents," she shouted,
"then be back here at two o'clock sharp for a Christmas
feast of feasts!" Goosey Gander honked his greeting, and
the two swooped back through the upstairs window,
coming to what sounded like a thumping, tumbling landing.
"I told you you could still do it, Goosey," Mother Goose
was heard to say. "Now, boys, we must fetch a big tree
and trim it. Quickly now. No time to waste."

When the villagers returned at two, they found the fat man and the stupid chap all spruced up and shiny. There was a great table on top of which were pork pies, chicken potpies, steak-and-kidney pies, pheasant pies, and mincemeat pies. There was a huge Christmas tree trimmed with every imaginable fruit tart and strung with

bright ribbons of cookies. "Oh, it's all so lovely," said Jack Sprat's wife. "Not a vegetable in sight."

"Again, a very Merry Christmas," said Mother Goose. "I've reopened The Queen of Hearts for you all. It's my Christmas present to you. We've been *too* long without a bakery shop. It was supposed to be a secret, but—"

"It *was* a secret," Jack Sprat interrupted.

"Good gracious!" said Mother Goose, "Just what did you think we were doing in here? No matter." She continued quickly, "Your Christmas present to me was the nicest I've ever received! While we were sweeping, scrubbing, and burning tons of trash and getting the ovens cleaned, your sweet carols made our work a joy."

"It surely was pretty," said the stupid one.

"I'm going to enjoy working here," said the fatty.

Mother Goose went on. "Now, then, let me explain. Last week I went to the fair at St. Ives to look for a pieman. I met a fine one. You'll see, as I did, once you taste his wares." She introduced the fat man. "I asked him how he would like a bakery shop of his own instead of his tiny stall on two wheels. He said it was the dream of his life, but that he would surely need a helper. Then along came Simple Simon here. Simple Simon wanted to buy a pie but hadn't a penny. I asked the pieman if he thought he could teach Simple Simon to be a helper. The pieman said the helper he had in mind should have a strong back, and that Simple Simon would surely do. Now it seems the dream of Simple Simon's life was to work in a bakery shop, so here we are.

"But I've talked enough. Let's be seated.

"Sit in the big chair, Humpty Dumpty. Oh, I say—you do seem to have pulled yourself together nicely! You sit by me, Little Miss Muffet—there's a sweet girl. All others, please find places.

"And Little Jack Horner, mind your table manners! Mustn't be sent to sit in the corner again.

"And now—LET'S EAT!"

Turn this page, please.

SOME OF THE CHARACTERS IN THIS BOOK AS SEEN BY MOTHER GOOSE

OLD MOTHER GOOSE

Old Mother Goose, when
    She wanted to wander,
Would ride through the air
    On a very fine gander.

LITTLE TOMMY TUCKER

Little Tommy Tucker
    Sings for his supper.
What shall he eat?
    White bread and butter.
How will he cut it
    Without e'er a knife?
How will he be married
    Without e'er a wife?

SIMPLE SIMON

Simple Simon met a pieman,
    Going to the fair;
Says Simple Simon to the pieman,
    "Let me taste your ware."

Says the pieman to Simple Simon,
    "Show me first your penny,"
Says Simple Simon to the pieman,
    "Indeed, I have not any."

LITTLE BOY BLUE

Little Boy Blue, come, blow your horn!
The sheep's in the meadow, the
    cow's in the corn.
Where's the little boy that looks
    after the sheep?
Under the haystack, fast asleep!

GEORGY PORGY

Georgy Porgy, pudding and pie,
Kissed the girls and made them cry.
When the boys came out to play,
Georgy Porgy ran away.

JACK AND JILL

Jack and Jill went up the hill,
    To fetch a pail of water;
Jack fell down, and broke his crown,
    And Jill came tumbling after.

MISS MUFFET

Little Miss Muffet
Sat on a tuffet,
Eating of curds and whey;
    There came a big spider,
    And sat down beside her,
And frightened Miss Muffet away.

LITTLE BO-PEEP

Little Bo-Peep has lost her sheep,
    And can't tell where to find them;
Leave them alone, and they'll come home,
    And bring their tails behind them.

HUMPTY DUMPTY

Humpty Dumpty sat on a wall,
Humpty Dumpty had a great fall;
All the King's horses, and all the King's men
Cannot put Humpty Dumpty together again.